Ray's
Violet

To Sophia, Audrey, + Timothy
I hope you enjoy
this story!

Sharon Walrond Harris

Ray's Violet

The Tale of a Most Extraordinary Lightning Bug

by
Sharon Walrond Harris

CreateSpace Independent Publishing Platform

This is a work of fiction. Names,
characters, places, and incidents are
a product of the author's imagination.
www.sharonwalrondharris.com

ISBN-13 978-1533490964
ISBN-10 1533490961

This book is dedicated
to my most
extraordinary
grandson, Gavin.

Contents

Chapter 1

House for Sale

Ray doesn't tell many people about Violet. When he told his mother, she laughed and said he had an unusual imagination. His dad thought it was a good joke. His friend, Adam, knows what happened, though, and so will those who read this story.

But Ray hopes they will keep it to themselves because he doesn't want people worrying about him any more than they already do.

It happened the summer after fourth grade in Indianapolis in the 1980s. This was a time when kids could play outside safely without parents having to worry too much about where they were or what they were doing.

Ray lived with his mom and dad and little sister, Sara. Their house was in a subdivision where the streets curve around in different directions forming a maze. A driver could get lost unless he lived there and knew which way to turn.

Ray's street ended in a court. He lived on one side of the circle and Adam's house was straight across. There were other children who lived in the court, too, but Adam had been Ray's best friend as long as he could remember.

It was a great place to live because there

wasn't very much traffic. The kids could play kickball in the court, and someone had even painted bases on the concrete, making a ball diamond right outside their front doors.

On the last day of school that year when Ray and Adam walked home together, they found a bright red sign in Ray's front yard that said "FOR SALE." Ray's summer was ruined on the first day.

Later, Ray asked his mom about the sign. His mother explained. "We lease this house. The realtor, Mr. Miller, who owns it, has decided to retire and move to Florida, and he doesn't want to have a rental house in Indiana to worry about."

"But, Mom," argued Ray, "this is our house. We've lived here for five years. This is the only house that I can remember."

"I know how you feel, Ray," she answered, "but it still belongs to Mr. Miller, and he can sell it if he wants to."

Ray asked his dad if they could buy the house themselves. "I think Mr. Miller is asking too much for it," his dad answered. "And besides, the prime lending interest rate has gone up three times in the last two months. That makes interest rates too high for us to afford a mortgage right now. But we'll find another house to rent that we like just as well. Don't worry. Everything will work out all right."

That explanation was confusing to Ray. He didn't know much about mortgages or interest rates, and his father's answer didn't help because he still worried. But he dared to hope that no one would buy it.

"Maybe interest rates will be too high for other people, too," Ray thought.

So that's how the summer began. Some days he could forget the house for a few hours, but then he would notice the sign and feel miserable again.

4

And then one day Ray found Violet. Or was it Violet who found Ray?

It was a typical day in the neighborhood. The boys had played kickball in the court, pitched horseshoes in Adam's backyard, and walked to the neighborhood grocery for candy. As they thought about what to do next, they realized it was almost time for supper.

"Better not mention that we just ate a candy bar," cautioned Adam.

"Right," said Ray, thinking of the lecture he'd get from his mom about spoiling his appetite. "Do you want to catch lightning bugs after supper?"

"Sure do. See you later." Adam headed across the court for home.

Summer evenings were as much fun as daytime in the court since most of the kids were allowed to stay out a while after dark.

They'd meet in one of their yards and

play games, tell scary stories, or just talk until someone's mom flashed her porch light off and on, which was the signal to come in. Ray hated to be the first to go in and could usually talk his mom into a little more time if she was the first to flash her porch light.

Later that evening, Ray and Adam prepared jars by punching air holes in the lids. They were standing in Ray's front yard as it grew dark, waiting to spot the first lightning bug.

"There's one," shouted Ray, running to a neighbor's yard trailing the flashing yellow light. "I've got it! Will you bring my jar to me?"

Adam found the jar in the grass and scrambled to where Ray was holding the bug cupped in his hands. Ray shoved it into the jar and quickly fastened the lid on the first capture of the night.

Other flashing lights were spotted, and the boys raced off in different directions.

Before long, they each had a small collection of lightning bugs to show for their efforts.

"I'm going to get one more and then quit," said Ray. "There's one."

"That's not a lightning bug," replied Adam. "I've never seen a purple lightning bug."

"But it's flashing like one," answered Ray. "Let's get it!"

The unusual insect did indeed have a purple light, and it seemed brighter than the other bugs—almost fluorescent. When they got closer, the boys were startled to hear a sound whenever the bug flashed. It was a soft tinkling sound like bells or metal wind chimes moving in the breeze, and it seemed to be coming from the bug.

It hovered over Ray's head as the boys watched and strained to listen. Then it slowly circled Ray's head. For a brief moment they seemed to communicate. Ray sensed immediately that the insect was a friendly creature.

The bug must have felt the same way about Ray, if such things are possible. It stopped circling, gently landed on Ray's outstretched arm, and sat there blinking, giving Ray the impression that it was smiling.

"Will you look at that!" whispered Adam. "Put it in your jar, quick."

"Let the other bugs go first," suggested Ray. "I don't want them anymore."

Adam emptied Ray's jar and handed it back to him. Ray carefully moved his arm toward the opening, slid the bug into it, and fastened the lid. The boys stood in amazement watching the purple flashes and listening to the faint sound.

Just then Ray saw another bright flash coming from behind him. He turned with a start and realized in relief that it was only his porch light flashing.

"I have to go in now. See you tomorrow,"

said Ray, carrying the jar with its unusual occupant toward the porch. He was so absorbed in watching the bug that he even forgot to ask his mom for extra time that night.

Chapter 2

The Disappearing Sandwich

L ying on his bed, Ray focused on the jar upon his dresser. He purposely left the room dark so he could watch the lightning bug, or whatever it was, light up. Every few seconds, the brilliant purple would appear, reminding him of a blinking neon sign, and each time he could hear the faint chiming sound. The pleasant light seemed to fill the room with a feeling of warmth. Instinctively, Ray felt that the bug was a girl, so he decided to call her Violet.

Ray got up and went to the kitchen for a snack. As he made a peanut butter and jelly sandwich, he wondered what Violet would eat. "I'll go to the library tomorrow to get a book about lightning bugs," he decided. "Maybe it will give me some ideas."

He carried the sandwich and a glass of milk back to his room and put them on the dresser. Then he turned on the light and opened the jar. Violet hesitated a moment, flew to the rim of the jar, and surveyed the room.

Just then, Ray heard his mother calling him from the kitchen. "Oh, oh. I know what she wants," he thought. "I left a mess."

He ran back to the kitchen, cleaned up,

and returned to his room. When he opened the door, he saw that Violet wasn't on the jar where he'd left her.

"Where are you, Violet girl?" he said aloud. Immediately, he heard the tinkling sound and spotted her light on the dresser where he'd put the sandwich.

"What happened to my sandwich?" he exclaimed. "It's gone! Violet, you didn't...you couldn't, could you? How could you eat a whole sandwich bigger than you are?"

Suddenly Violet's light blinked on and off rapidly and her sounds blended into what sounded like merry laughter. "She's laughing," thought Ray. "She did eat it!"

Violet flew straight up and landed on Ray's nose, flashing and tinkling in a very contented manner. "Well, what do you know!" exclaimed Ray aloud, staring cross-eyed at his new pet.

When Ray reluctantly began to get ready

for bed at his mother's insistence, he wondered what to do with Violet for the night. His first thought was to put her back into the jar, but she put up such a fuss that he stopped. Her message came through. She did not want to go into the jar, and she was letting Ray know it.

Amazed at this unusual creature, Ray stared as Violet made a tour of his room. In one corner was a fluffy stuffed dog about three feet tall that Ray had bought at a garage sale. Violet hovered over it, seemed to approve, and settled onto a spot between its ears.

"O.K., Violet," said Ray as he turned out the light and climbed into bed. "I couldn't have picked a better place for you myself."

Ray's mind was filled with the events of the evening, and as he drifted off to sleep, he seemed to hear the distant music of wind chimes in the breeze.

Chapter 3

The Magic Bowl of Popcorn

Ray awakened to the sound of his parents eating breakfast in the kitchen. At first, he couldn't recall what was different. Then he remembered. The lightning bug—Violet! He jumped up and looked at the stuffed dog where she'd settled down last night. She wasn't there. He searched his room but Violet was not to be found.

Running into the hallway toward the kitchen, Ray heard his father's voice exclaim, "What happened to my piece of toast? I just took one bite before I got up to get some coffee. Now it's gone. Where's my toast?"

All at once Ray knew what happened to the toast. Peering through the doorway, his eyes searched the kitchen in one sweep without spotting Violet. More carefully this time, he scanned the room until his attention was attracted by a slight movement on top of a picture frame behind his father. There sat Violet looking very self-satisfied.

"Morning, Ray. Come on in," said his father chuckling. "So, you took my toast! Playing tricks this early in the morning, are you? Peeking around the corner to see my reaction? Sandra, I told you this boy is becoming a practical joker."

"Dad," said Ray hesitantly. "I think my purple lightning bug ate your toast."

Ray's father roared with laughter as he put another piece of bread in the toaster. "You're right about his imagination, Sandra. That's a good one, Ray. Sit down and have some more breakfast. Purple lightning bug! Ha, ha, ha!"

Ray sat down with a sigh. It would be no use to tell them about Violet. They would just think he was making it up. During breakfast, Ray kept an eye on Violet perched on the picture frame. He couldn't wait to tell Adam about all she had done.

His dad soon left for work, and his mother went to her room to change out of her robe. As Ray carried his dishes to the sink, he wondered how to get Violet back to his room. He was surprised when she flew down to his shoulder as if she entirely understood the situation.

Later, in his front yard, Ray found Adam waiting impatiently for him to come out. He told Adam all that had happened.

"She eats peanut butter and jelly sandwiches? And toast? Wow!" exclaimed Adam. "And the name

Violet fits her. She seems to understand what's going on."

"She sure does." said Ray. "Hey, let's ask if you can spend the night with me tonight, and we can watch her."

The boys kept themselves busy that day with their usual games, interrupting their play periodically to run into Ray's room to check on Violet. She seemed content to spend the time exploring the room, and she obviously took great pleasure in pestering Ray's two parakeets, Patti and Blue Boy, who lived in a cage in the room.

They became agitated and chirped noisily whenever Violet came close. She was able to zip in and out of the cage before they could get to her, and Ray suspected she was snatching their food and water. He went to the kitchen and got a bowl of water for Violet, glad to learn more about what she needed.

Ray's parents agreed to let him invite Adam to stay overnight, so after supper the boys went to

Ray's room. Violet seemed glad to have company and flew from one boy to the other, flashing and tinkling gleefully. They found that when they held out a hand, she would land on it seeming to giggle.

Later, as they played a game of cards, Ray realized he was hungry. "I'd like something to eat. How about you?"

"Yeah, some popcorn would sure be good," agreed Adam.

Immediately, Violet, who had been resting on Ray's shoulder, began flashing strangely and making a noise they hadn't heard before. It was a series of buzzing sounds, some longer than others, and her light blinked in coordination with them. The boys stared in amazement. Then she stopped as suddenly as she had started and resumed her nap.

"What was that all about?" gasped Ray.

"You know what?" said Adam. "She sounded just like an old fashioned telegraph like they had out West in the old days. I saw one on a cowboy show on TV."

19

A short while later, there was a knock on the door. Ray's mother came in carrying a large bowl of buttered popcorn and two glasses of soda. "I thought you boys might like a snack," she said.

"Thanks, Mom!" exclaimed Ray. "We were just talking about popcorn." Suddenly the boys looked at one another in astonishment, the same idea forming in both their minds.

"You know," explained Ray's mother. "I was reading a book when I heard a buzzing in my ears, and then I had a sudden craving for popcorn. I couldn't continue reading until I went to the kitchen and made some. So, here it is, hot out of the popper. Strangest thing." She went back to the living room and her own bowl of popcorn.

As soon as the door closed behind her, Violet began to flash and chime in the way that Ray recognized as laughter. "She's laughing, Adam!" Ray shouted. "She did it! Somehow she gave my mother the idea to make popcorn."

"The telegraph sound! She started that right

after I mentioned popcorn," said Adam. "Could she have been sending a message? That's impossible, isn't it, Ray?"

"I don't know what's possible and what isn't anymore," said Ray.

Chapter 4

The Library Escapade

The next morning, the boys ate breakfast and saved a piece of toast for Violet. Then they walked to a branch library several blocks away. Ray asked the librarian to help them look for a book about lightning bugs. She checked the catalogue card file but didn't find anything listed.

"We'll have to look under 'insect books'," she said. She found quite a few of those, so she showed the boys where to locate them and how to look in the index for "fireflies," as lightning bugs are called.

Ray selected two books and was excited to go home to read them.

Adam suggested they look for a book about the early telegraph since Violet sounded so much like one. The librarian found one in the card file called *The Talking Wires*.

"This is great! Thanks," said Adam .

"You're very welcome, young man," the librarian answered, as if making a speech. "It's wonderful to see young people interested in reading. Too many children these days waste their time watching television all day long. What a dreadful waste of time when all these books are waiting to be read." She swept her hand dramatically around the library pointing to the shelves.

As the librarian was checking out their books

at the front desk, Ray suddenly heard a familiar tinkling sound. He turned around just in time to see a man who was reading a magazine swat at something around his head. Then Ray heard it again—Violet's laughter!

His eyes frantically searched for Violet, and there she was, perched on a bookshelf, flashing and tinkling in her merry way. When the man began to read again, she hopped from the shelf and hovered by his ear. She seemed to enjoy her little joke.

"Look! It's Violet!" whispered Ray. "How do you suppose she got here?"

"She must have come with us," answered Adam. Then he spotted Ray's baseball cap lying on a table where he'd put it when they entered the library. "She must have been in your cap."

To the boys' horror, Violet now flew over to the check-out desk and settled onto a stack of returned books. "Oh! A bug in my library!" gasped the librarian. "Mabel, where's the fly swatter?" she shrieked to her assistant.

"Right here, Miss Sprinkle," answered Mabel, handing her a well-worn fly swatter.

Miss Sprinkle took the swatter in hand and turned toward Violet, looking like a soldier going into battle. Whack! It came down onto the books as Violet escaped just in time.

Violet hovered above Miss Sprinkle's head as the librarian continued to swish the swatter through the air as if in combat.

It was obvious to the boys that Violet was having fun. She made her laughing sound as she avoided each swing of the swatter.

"Mabel, help me!" cried Miss Sprinkle.

The assistant picked up a magazine from the desk and charged toward Violet. The two ladies waved their weapons back and forth, while Violet danced up and down, in and out, dodging the blows.

"We've got to get Violet out of here," whispered Ray urgently. "What'll we do?"

"Get your cap," suggested Adam. "Maybe

she'll go back into it."

Just then, Violet came to rest on top of Miss Sprinkle's head. Mabel stepped up onto a chair to better reach the bug.

"Don't move," shouted Mabel. "I've got it!"

The magazine came down with a whack on Miss Sprinkle's head, knocking her glasses to the floor. At the same moment, Mabel lost her balance, grabbed for Miss Sprinkle's arm to steady herself, and came tumbling down. Mabel was not a small person, and the force of her fall pushed Miss Sprinkle down under her. The two librarians fell to the floor in a heap.

Meanwhile, Violet dodged the magazine, flew to Ray's shoulder and sat there giggling. The boys muttered "thank you" to the librarians, grabbed their books, and hurried out the door.

Chapter 5

Plumbing Problems

When they got back to Ray's house with Violet safely inside the cap, his mother was vacuuming. Switching off the sweeper, she said, "Ray, I'm glad you're home. I want you to make your bed and straighten your room. I'll be in there to vacuum in a few minutes.

The realtor, Mr. Miller, is going to show the house this afternoon. He's bringing a family that is moving to town and looking for a house to buy."

This was terrible news. Ray didn't like to clean his room, but that was not the worst part. Someone might buy their house. They would have to move—and soon. Suddenly he felt miserable. He dropped his books onto a chair and headed toward his room.

"See you later, Ray," said Adam, taking his book and going home.

In his room, Ray opened the cap to let Violet free. She flew to her water dish for a drink, evidently thirsty after her morning escapade. She perched on the dresser and watched Ray pick up his things and stuff them into drawers and the closet.

"What's going to happen, Violet?" asked Ray, talking more to himself than to her. "What if these people like the house, and we have to move? I'll never see my friends again."

Violet began flashing as if to answer his question. He glanced at her in surprise. She seemed to be talking to him, but he had no idea what she might be trying to say.

Then Ray heard the vacuum cleaner approaching, and he hurried to pick up the rest of his things. He was making his bed when his mother turned into his room and shut off the sweeper.

"Well, your room doesn't look too bad now," she said. "Pull the bedspread a little smoother. You might get the hang of making beds after all. Do I dare look in your closet?"

"I don't think you'd better," muttered Ray. "I stuffed a lot of things in there. Those people aren't going to look in the closets, are they? Boy, you don't get any privacy when your house is for sale."

"Let's hope they don't look in yours, at least," answered his mother. "There isn't time to clean it out now. Ray, I'd like you to run over to the store to get some laundry soap. I used the last of it yesterday, and I want to wash the kitchen curtains before the people come. They're looking a little dingy. And Ray, when you get back, please take a quick bath and change clothes."

"Aw, Mom! They're coming to look at the house, not me."

"Now, Ray. It won't hurt you to clean up a bit. Please don't argue with me and run to the store."

"All right," groaned Ray. He knew from the tone of her voice that it was no use to disagree.

He glanced at Violet. She was resting on the shelf behind his electronic football game and seemed to have fallen asleep. He thought she'd be safe there, so he took the money his mother handed him and hurried out to the store.

Ray got home in good time with the detergent. He went to his room to check on Violet and get ready for his bath. She was just where he'd left her. When he spoke, she moved slightly and flashed a greeting.

"Violet, I have to take a bath now. The people will be here soon. I hope they won't like the house.

At least if we have to move, I can take you with me."

He took Violet into the bathroom and began running his bath. Closing the drain in the tub, he turned on the water full force and adjusted the hot and cold until the temperature was just right. He undressed, got in the tub, and waited for it to fill. His mind was full of dreary thoughts about starting a new life with no friends in a strange school.

Suddenly, Violet, who was perched on top of the mirror, began her strange buzzing with a pattern of long and short sounds. Ray watched her for about a minute, and then she stopped as suddenly as she had started.

Just then Ray realized that the water was beginning to rise near the top of the tub. He liked to have the tub full, and his mother often complained that he used too much water, but now it was getting too full. He turned both faucets to "off," and they moved easily—too easily—but the water did not stop. He tried again, moving the handles back and forth, but the water continued to run. It was dangerously near the rim now, threatening to overflow.

Ray grabbed the drain knob and pulled up sharply, but nothing happened. He tried again, but it was no use. Nothing changed the forceful flow of water into the tub.

He jumped out of the tub, wrapped himself in a towel, and yelled for his mom just as the water topped the rim and began to overflow onto the floor. "Mom, Help!"

His mother came rushing into the bathroom. "What's the matter? Oh, no!" she gasped when she saw the water streaming over the side of the tub. "Turn off the water!"

"I can't," answered Ray. "The faucets turn but the water won't stop. The drain won't open either. What'll we do?"

She reached for the faucet and tried to turn it off, but it had no effect on the water overflowing onto the floor.

"Oh, my goodness!" she cried. "The realtor

will be here soon. I guess I'll have to call a plumber."

She ran to the kitchen and had just picked up the phone book to find a plumber when she spotted more water. It was running into the kitchen from the laundry room. She dropped the phone book and ran to see what was wrong. The washing machine was overflowing, too. She pushed the dials, but just like in the bathtub, they didn't work. The water continued to run out onto the floor.

"Oh, my goodness!" she gasped. "Ray! Sara! Get all the towels you can find and put them down to soak up the water. I've got to call a plumber."

Ray grabbed all the rest of the towels from the linen closet, and Sara came running from her room to help spread them on the floor. The towels were soon soaked through, and the water kept coming.

Just then there was a knock at the front door. Ray's mother finished her call, hung up the phone, and went to the door, looking as if she might faint.

"Good afternoon, Mrs. Wright," said Mr.

Miller in a business-like voice. "I know we're here early. I hope it's not inconvenient. This is Mr. and Mrs. Johnson. They would like to see the house."

"Oh, yes," said Mrs. Johnson. "From the outside it looks just like what we need."

"Well, uh," began Ray's mother hesitantly. "We seem to be having a little problem here. I've just called a plumber. He'll be here soon."

"Oh? Is there a faucet dripping or something?" asked the realtor. "We can just overlook that. A new rubber washer and it'll be good as new."

"Well, uh, I wouldn't exactly call it a drip," answered Mrs. Wright. "It's more like a..."

"A flood!" shouted Ray from the bathroom.

"Well, you see, the faucets won't turn off, and the drain won't open, and the washing machine won't stop, and the water is running all over the floor, and I've called the plumber, and he'll be here soon," blurted out Ray's mother. "If you could come back in a couple of hours, I'm sure we'll have it fixed and all cleaned up."

Mr. and Mrs. Johnson were already turning to go to their car. "No, thank you!" said Mr. Johnson. "We don't want to see any more. We had enough plumbing problems in our old house. I'm not about to buy another house with plumbing problems."

The realtor followed the Johnsons to their car trying to explain that it was surely something minor and could be easily fixed, but their minds were made up. They all got into their cars and drove away, just as the plumber's truck turned into the court.

At dinner that evening, Ray's mother was explaining to his father what happened. "And then," she went on, "the plumber said there was nothing wrong. He just turned the faucets and the water stopped. He pulled the knob and the drain opened. And he pushed the dial on the washing machine, and it stopped. We tried and tried and couldn't stop the water, and the plumber just turned it off. I never felt so silly in all my life. I just don't understand what happened."

Ray hadn't understood either, until he remembered Violet and went to look for her. She was still on top of the bathroom mirror. When she saw Ray, she flashed so happily that he realized what had happened. He remembered her buzzing sounds and knew that somehow she had caused it to happen.

He had learned that she was mischievous, but it surprised him that she'd do something like this. Later, it was Adam who understood.

"Don't you see, Ray?" he asked. "She was helping you! She must know that you don't want to move, and she did it to make the people dislike the house. It didn't really cause any permanent damage, did it?"

"No," answered Ray. "After we got everything mopped up and dried out, it was fine. It was a pretty good idea, wasn't it? They didn't even want to look at the house when they heard about the water.

But it's still for sale. I can't expect her to do that every time someone comes to look at it."

"Yeah," replied Adam, "but at least you have a little more time now."

Chapter 6

All About Fireflies

The next day, the boys read their library books hoping to find out more about Violet. The more they read, the more they began to think she wasn't a lightning bug at all—at least, not a typical one.

"Look here," said Ray. "This says that a firefly is not a fly but a beetle. It says their lights are yellow or yellowish green. It doesn't mention a purple light at all. And it says that females don't fly very much, and some species of females don't even have wings. They stay on the ground or in low bushes. The males are the ones who fly around flashing."

"That doesn't sound anything like Violet," replied Adam.

"Maybe she is not a firefly," said Ray. "The book says that fireflies eat mainly snails and worms. That's when they're in the larva stage and aren't lightning bugs yet. It says most adult fireflies don't even eat at all."

"That's not Violet. She'll eat anything she can get close to," remarked Adam. "Cookies, toast, popcorn, birdseed—you name it, she'll eat it."

"You can say that again! Hey, wait a minute," said Ray. "At the end of this part it says, 'Surprisingly little is known about the habits of fireflies.' Maybe they don't know yet that there's a purple species that makes chiming sounds when it flashes."

"Oh, sure. We'll be famous as the ones who discovered the purple, flashing, tinkling, mind-reading, anything-eating whatchamacallit! I can see the headlines now," said Adam, pretending to hold an imaginary newspaper.

"Well, at least she's not a purple-people-eater."

"Maybe she is!" gasped Adam. "She's just being friendly so she can eat us! Aah!" he screamed, clutching his throat.

"Ooh, save me!" Ray chimed in, falling on the bed, laughing.

"The purple-people-eater is after us!" chortled Adam, collapsing in a fit of giggling.

Violet, who was sleeping on the stuffed dog, woke up when the laughing began. She seemed to understand, as usual, and must have wanted to get in on the game, because she began to dive at the boys, making a buzzing sound. She seemed to pretend to be a purple-people-eater trying to get them.

There was a quick knock at the door, and Sara came in. "What's going on in here?" she asked. "You boys are making so much noise I can hardly hear my TV show." She stopped suddenly as she saw Violet diving and landing on Ray's head.

"What's that?" she yelled.

"Ah, it's nothing," said Ray.

"It's just an old lightning bug we found," added Adam.

"But lightning bugs aren't purple." Sara walked closer to get a better look, and Violet flashed and hovered in front of her.

Ray quickly shut the door. "Sara, it's a secret. This is Violet, my purple...something. She's like a lightning bug, but not exactly. She's my pet."

Adam explained, "She understands what we say. And she can laugh, and she eats any kind of food. She can read our minds."

"And do magic things," continued Ray.

"You guys are kidding me," said Sara. "You're just making it up. Bugs can't do things like that."

"This one can," said Ray. "She's trying to help us. She made the water overflow from the bathtub and the washing machine."

"Oh, she did not," said Sara. "That's impossible."

"Well, don't you think it's strange that when the plumber came, he just turned the water off when we couldn't turn it off before?" asked Ray.

Adam said, "Violet has a way of buzzing like a telegraph that makes things happen."

"She gave Mother the idea to make popcorn one night," added Ray.

"Did you tell Mom and Dad?" asked Sara.

"I tried to tell them about my purple lightning bug one time," Ray explained, "but Dad just thought it was a joke. They won't believe us. It was hard for Adam and me to believe it until we saw what she can do."

Sara stayed to play with Violet and grew to like her as much as the boys did. She promised to keep the secret.

Chapter 7

Sending Messages

The next day, Adam came over excited about what he'd read in his book about the telegraph. He explained that electrical impulses were sent through wires to a receiver at the other end. They used a code of dots and dashes called Morse Code. A dot was a short sound and a dash was three times as long.

The book had a Morse Code alphabet, and the

boys practiced writing each other notes in code, using the book to translate the message. They soon knew some of the letters by heart.

"Do you think the noises Violet made were really Morse Code?" asked Ray.

"Sounded like it to me. Let's try to send her a message," said Adam.

They decided that if Violet would do something they told her to do in a message, they could be sure that she understood. They worked out the dots and dashes for "fly to the dresser."

"You go first," said Ray, so Adam began to make the sounds, and they watched Violet to see what she would do. Suddenly she flashed and tinkled her laughing sound, as if amused at Adam's clumsy efforts at Morse Code. Then she slowly rose into the air and flew to the top of the dresser, still giggling.

Ray and Adam stared at each other. "She did it!" shouted Ray. "Violet knows Morse Code."

They wrote another message. This time they told her to go to the curtain rod. Ray took a turn sounding the dots and dashes, and he had finished only the first word when Violet flew from the dresser to the curtain rod.

"She didn't let me finish." said Ray. "She knew what I was going to say before I was done."

Violet flew down onto Ray's head and

started buzzing.

"Now she's doing it!" shouted Ray. "Listen. She's sending a message."

"I think I heard an 'e'," said Adam. "That's easy because it's only one dot."

"We'll have to write it down. Say it again, Violet, and go slower. We're new at this," instructed Ray.

Violet began again, and Ray wrote down the dots and dashes. When she finished, she waited for them to decode the message from the book.

"It says, 'Clap your hands.' What kind of a message is that?" wondered Ray.

"She's just doing what we did," explained Adam. "Do what she says."

They clapped their hands, and Violet danced around in the air laughing merrily. She seemed pleased that they had understood and was willing to play the game as long as they wanted. By buzzing messages, she told Adam to stand on his head and Ray to turn a somersault. She told them to sing a song, so they sang "Row, Row, Row Your Boat," while Violet flashed in time to the beat.

The next message snapped them out of their playful mood in a hurry. They read, "The realtor is coming again."

Chapter 8

Another Family Visits

"Violet," urged Ray, "think of something quick! What can we do this time to make them not want the house?"

But Violet had already flown to her resting place between the ears of the stuffed dog and seemed to be sleeping, although every so often the boys noticed her purplish light pulsate ever so slightly.

"What a time to take a nap!" groaned Adam.

As the boys walked from Ray's room into the hall the telephone rang, and they heard Ray's mother answer it.

"Oh, hello Mr. Miller. Yes," his mother was saying, "the plumber came. No, we haven't had any more problems with the water. I can't imagine what was wrong, but it's working well now. Oh...yes, four o'clock would be fine. We'll see you then. Good-by."

"Ray, Sara," his mother called. "The realtor is bringing another family to see the house at four o'clock. Please straighten your rooms again. And Ray, you don't have to take a bath this time. We don't want to take any chances. In fact, don't anyone turn on the water until they've gone."

"Mom, you don't think the same thing would happen again, do you?" asked Sara, walking from the kitchen eating a cookie.

"Oh, of course not," sighed Mrs. Wright. "I'm

just a little nervous. I'd hate to try to explain to Mr. Miller if something like that happened again. Don't drop any crumbs, Sara. Let's get busy, both of you."

She clapped her hands two times. The kids knew that meant, "No fooling around; get busy!"

As Adam was leaving for home, he glanced at Ray. They exchanged a knowing look, but Ray appeared worried. Would Violet help them again, or was it just a coincidence that the water overflowed last time?

"See ya later, Ray. Come outside after supper if you can," said Adam, closing the screen door.

By four o'clock the children had finished their jobs, and Ray sat on the front porch wondering how Violet had known that the realtor was going to call. There were new surprises every day. Now they could communicate with her by Morse Code, and she could tell things that were going to happen in the future. What would be next?

Ray went to his room to get Violet so that the visitors wouldn't see her. He walked over to the stuffed dog, but Violet wasn't there. He looked on his dresser, in the jar, on the curtain rod, and even under his bed, but he couldn't find Violet anywhere.

Ray heard a knock on the door. They were here. He listened uneasily as his mother greeted Mr. Miller and the prospective buyers. Mr. Miller introduced the family, and Ray began to hear many kids' voices. His curiosity got the better of him, and he went into the hall, peering around the corner into the living room.

There stood a very big man, a tiny little lady, and five children. Ray guessed that the oldest was about ten years old and the youngest about two. He immediately disliked all of them. The thought of them living in his house, sleeping in his bedroom, and playing in his court made him feel sad.

When his mother said, "And this is my son, Ray," he muttered, "Hello," and worked his way through the crowd to the front door and out onto the porch. He sat there feeling dejected while they looked through the house.

He had begun to hope that something would go wrong again like last time. But the plumbing hadn't acted up, and everything was in tip-top shape. And now he couldn't find Violet. He thought that he and Adam must have let their imaginations run wild about Violet. Those things couldn't possibly have happened.

Just then the visitors emerged through the front door. The children ran into the yard, giggling and slamming the screen door behind them.

"That big boy will probably be Adam's next best friend," thought Ray. Then Ray snapped to attention when he overheard the man talking to the realtor as they walked to their cars. Ray strained to listen, and his heart began to pound in excitement.

"It's a nice house, Mr. Miller," the man was saying, "but I'm afraid it just won't do for us. We've got to have more room with these young-uns—at least four bedrooms and a family room. I hope the next one you're going to show us is bigger."

"Mom!" Ray burst through the doorway into

the house. "Mom, they don't want it! They're not going to buy the house! It's too small. Yippee!"

With the immediate danger of having to move passed, at least for the time being, Ray turned his attention to Violet. He spent the next hour searching every room in the house, trying not to be obvious about it. When he got to Sara's room, she insisted that her room was private, and he was not allowed to go in without permission.

"What do you want in my room, anyway?" yelled Sara.

"Shhh," whispered Ray. "Stop yelling and listen. I can't find Violet. She's not anywhere else in the house. Maybe she flew into your room."

So the children searched Sara's room from top to bottom, but Violet was not there. Ray lost hope of finding her. He suddenly felt very alone. Why would she leave, just when he was getting to know her? It didn't make sense. But then, nothing in the last few days had made any sense.

Ray heard the telephone ring. His mother

answered and said, "Oh, hi Pat. No, I guess they didn't like the house. Ray heard them say it was too small."

Pat was Adam's mother. She and his mother were friends and talked on the phone occasionally, so Ray was only mildly interested in their conversation.

There was a tap at the front screen door, and Adam motioned Ray outside.

"You're not going to believe this," whispered Adam. "Violet's at my house!"

Chapter 9

The Last Visit

"I don't know how she got to my house," explained Adam. "When I got home, I turned on the television to watch cartoons. I kept hearing a chiming sound. At first, I thought it was part of the music on TV, but I realized it sounded like Violet, and it was right by my ear. There she was on my shoulder, flashing and chiming!"

"Whew! I'm glad she's safe. I thought she was gone forever," exclaimed Ray. "Where is she now?"

"She's in my room. I gave her some water and a piece of bread, and she was sleeping on my pillow when I left," explained Adam. "But something strange happened," he continued.

"That's not unusual when Violet's around," said Ray, relieved that she was up to her usual tricks. "What happened?"

"Well," began Adam, "I started to reach for her on my shoulder, but she flew away and went straight into the kitchen. She landed on the window sill behind my mom, who was sitting at the table writing a letter."

"Oh, no!" exclaimed Ray. "Did your mom see her?"

"No, but I thought she would hear her," sighed Adam, "because Violet started that Morse Code buzzing right there behind her head."

"Wow! Could you figure out the message?"

"No, she went too fast. But here's the strangest part. My mom looked up from her letter like she was thinking about something, and then she went to the phone and called my Aunt Rita. Aunt Rita got her real estate license a couple of months ago and just got a job selling houses. Mom asked her questions about buying a house without getting a new mor--, a new mortar or something like that."

"Mortgage," said Ray. "I've heard a lot about mortgages and interest rates and stuff lately. It all has to do with how you buy a house."

"Boy, I hope that doesn't mean that we're going to move, too. Anyway," continued Adam, "they hung up, but then Aunt Rita called back a few minutes later, and then my mom called your mom. That's when I took Violet to my room and came over here to tell you."

"Gee, thanks, Adam. I'll come over after supper and get her, okay?"

"Sure. See ya later." Adam turned and ran across the court.

When Ray's father came home after work, Ray was helping his mother with supper, and Sara was setting the table.

"Hi, Dad," said Ray. "Some people looked at the house today, but they didn't like it. It's too small for them and all their giggly kids. We lucked out again."

"Ray, someone is going to buy the house eventually," cautioned his father, "so don't get your hopes up about staying. We'll start looking for houses to rent this weekend. We might even find one we like better than this one."

"No, we won't," thought Ray. "My friends won't be there."

While the family was eating supper, Ray's mother explained about the phone call. "John, Pat from across the street called today. You know, Adam's mother. Her sister is in real estate, and she said that sometimes people can buy houses on contract if the owner is willing to sell it that way. You don't have to get a new mortgage. You make payments to the owner instead of to a mortgage company, and you often don't need to have a big down payment. Pat said she wasn't sure why she thought of telling me about that, but maybe the information could be useful to us. John, do you think Mr. Miller would want to sell this house on contract?"

"Oh, probably not," answered Ray's father. "I think he wants to move to Florida. He probably wants to get all his money out of it at once. I might mention it to him some time, though, and see what he says."

"Really?" Ray almost shouted. "We might be able to buy the house ourselves?"

"No, Ray, I said probably not. He still wants too much for it and probably doesn't want to sell it on contract, anyway. So don't get your hopes up," his dad cautioned again.

After supper, Ray went to Adam's house to

get Violet. She seemed very glad to see him and flashed and chimed all the way home as if she were singing.

Three days later the realtor called again. He asked to bring another family to look at the house. When they arrived, Ray began to worry all over again. They were a young couple with only one child, a little girl about four years old.

"This house would be just fine for them. They'd have plenty of room," thought Ray.

The small family walked through the house slowly. Ray sat in the living room listening to their comments coming from the bedrooms.

He heard the little girl pick which room she wanted for her own. He heard the mother say how nicely their furniture would fit into the house. He could tell that the father was impressed with the fenced-in back yard and the large maple tree. He heard them say that the yard would be perfect for the puppy that the little girl had been promised as soon as they found a house.

Ray's heart sank as he watched them leave. They talked excitedly with Mr. Miller as they stood by their car for at least ten minutes, glancing at the house from time to time.

Ray went to find Violet, who had been resting in one of his dresser drawers during their visit. When Ray opened the drawer, she seemed to be sleeping contentedly without a care in the world.

"Violet," Ray said sadly. "I think those people like the house, and they are probably going to buy it."

He lay down on his bed and stared at the ceiling. "It's no use hoping anymore," he sighed. I guess I knew it would happen sometime."

Violet began to buzz and flash a Morse Code message, but Ray's eyes were feeling heavy. He rolled over on his bed and fell asleep without writing down the dots and dashes of Violet's message.

Mr. Miller called again that evening. He told Ray's mother that the same family would like to look at the house again tomorrow. He said they had narrowed their choices to two houses, but he thought they liked this one best. He explained that he hoped they would buy it, because he and his wife were anxious to move to Florida, and he wanted to finalize the sale before they moved. He made an appointment for two o'clock.

Since the next day was Saturday, Ray's father didn't have to work and was at home. This time, when Ray opened the drawer for Violet, she wouldn't go in. She flew out of Ray's reach and seemed to be playing. Ray gave up trying to get her into the drawer, and she finally came to rest on his shoulder as Mr. Miller knocked on the door.

Ray was still in his room when he heard the visitors go into the kitchen. Suddenly Violet flashed and buzzed.

"Not now, Violet!" whispered Ray in alarm. "They'll hear you."

Then Ray heard the lady say from the kitchen, "I think I need more cabinets than this, Walter. The other house has more."

As the family went into the living room, Violet continued buzzing, and the lady complained again.

"I had forgotten that this carpet is brown. I like the green carpet in the other house better," she said.

When they started to come toward the bedrooms, Ray slipped through the back way to the kitchen with Violet so they wouldn't hear her. Then he heard the lady say, "You know, Walter, the other house has more closet space. And this one has only one bathroom. The other one has two."

The man said, "I did like the fireplace in the other house. Mr. Miller, we'll take it—the other one. Let us know when you have the papers ready to sign. Good-by, Mr. and Mrs. Wright. Thank you."

They walked out the front door to their car. Immediately Violet stopped buzzing. She chimed and flashed in her laughing way, and Ray realized that Violet had done it again.

Chapter 10

Anything's Possible

Mr. Miller didn't leave with the others this time. Ray could hear him talking to his mom and dad. "My wife is hoping to leave for Florida next month," he was saying, "but we won't be able to go until I can sell this house. I just can't seem to find a buyer; something always goes wrong. I thought this family wanted it, and then they changed their minds just like that."

Ray held his breath as he heard his father offer to buy the house if Mr. Miller could lower the price and would be willing to sell it on contract.

"Mr. Wright," the realtor answered, "I wouldn't have considered that a month ago, but now I'm practically desperate. You have a deal! I'll get the paperwork together and come back Monday evening to sign the contract. It'll be a load off my mind!"

And so it was settled, just like that. What had seemed impossible was now true. Ray would not have to go to a new school or leave his friends. He would not have to move.

Later, sitting on the porch, Ray told Adam all about how Violet had made the people choose the other house and how his dad had offered to buy the house and Mr. Miller accepted his offer.

"And we're going to sign the papers on Monday," said Ray. "It's hard to believe that I won't be worrying about moving anymore."

"It's even harder to believe that a lightning bug made your wish come true," marveled Adam. "And a purple one at that!"

"Yeah," sighed Ray. "I don't try to understand it, because it doesn't make any sense. I just know that things you think are impossible aren't always impossible. They can happen."

"Ray, I just thought of something!" Adam was growing excited. "You have a gold mine there. Violet, I mean. Think of what else she could get for you, and maybe me, too. The sky's the limit. Nothing's impossible, remember?"

"Wow!" exclaimed Ray. "I bet she could help us hit a home run in a baseball game!"

"Of course she could," agreed Adam. "And what about getting our parents to raise our allowance?"

"Or help us get good grades in school," added Ray.

"Yeah, and what about that new bike you

want?" asked Adam. "That'd be a snap for her."

"Great idea! Let's go tell Violet." The boys ran to Ray's room. Violet was teasing the parakeets again, and they were chattering angrily. She flew from one boy to the other, landing on Ray's shoulder.

When the boys asked Violet about helping Ray to get a new bike, she must have found the request funny, because she began to dance around their heads, flashing and tinkling, and then she started buzzing a message.

"Quick, Adam. Write this down." They used the library book to decode the message, and they read, "Follow me."

Violet hovered a few feet in front of them and moved out of the room, down the hall, and through the living room to the front door.

"She wants to go outside," said Adam. "Maybe she is going to lead us to the bike." The boys followed Violet down Ray's sidewalk. Then she went to the corner, turned right, and continued leading them for three blocks. She stopped in front of a house where two elderly ladies lived.

"Why did we come here, Violet?" asked Ray. "Do they have the bike?" Violet flew to Ray's shoulder and sat there without a sound. Ray noticed the ladies in their side yard. They walked toward the boys.

One of the ladies said, "Just look at how tall this grass is. Do you boys cut grass? The boy we had moved away, and we haven't found anyone else to cut the grass yet."

"We'd be glad to pay you," said the other lady. "You'd be doing us a favor. We've got to get this yard back into shape!"

"Well," answered Ray. "I cut the grass at my house sometimes, and Adam cuts his. I guess we could cut yours."

"Oh, wonderful," exclaimed the first lady. "Come around early Monday morning, and we'll get started. If you do a good job, we'll pay you well, and you can cut it every week."

When the ladies went inside, Violet again started leading the boys. They followed her to a house around the block.

"O.K., Violet, what are we doing here?" asked Ray. "Is this where the bike is?"

"Ray," sighed Adam. "Do you notice anything about this yard?"

Ray looked around the yard. "No, nothing special, except some flowers and a tree. No bike."

"The grass!" shouted Adam. "Look at the grass."

"Oh, no." groaned Ray. "It's too tall. Are you thinking what I'm thinking? She wants us to offer to cut the grass."

Adam nodded. Violet flashed and tinkled happily and led the boys to the door. Ray knocked on the door. A man leaning on a pair of crutches opened it.

Ray asked, "Would you like someone to cut your grass?"

"I sure would," said the man. "I hurt my foot

last week, and I'm not going to be able to cut it for quite a while. I'll be glad to pay you to mow every week."

The boys were beginning to understand what Violet was trying to tell them. Before they returned home, they had three more mowing jobs for next week, and most of the people wanted them to cut their grass every week for the rest of the summer.

The boys discussed what had happened. "She wants me to earn the money for my bike," said Ray.

"Yup," agreed Adam. "She sounds just like my mom and dad."

"I never heard your mom and dad tinkle like a wind chime," laughed Ray.

"Oh, you know what I mean. Not the sound—the idea. 'Earn the money for things you want. You'll appreciate them more if you work for them.' " said Adam, mimicking an adult.

"I think I'd appreciate a bike if Violet gave it to me," said Ray. "But she did help us get a lot of mowing jobs. I should be able to save enough money for a bike before the summer is over."

"Me, too," agreed Adam.

The next evening, the boys planned their jobs for the week. They made a chart listing each job, the address, and the day they would do it. Violet had been resting quietly while they worked, but suddenly she flew up, circled around them, and buzzed a message.

Adam reached for a pencil and wrote it down while Ray looked up the code. "Where there's a will, there's a way," it read.

"What do you think that is supposed to mean, Adam?"

Adam repeated it, " 'Where there's a will, there's a way.' I guess it means if you want something badly enough, there will always be a way to make it happen."

"Yeah," said Ray. "Like cutting grass to earn money for a bike."

Then Violet flashed another message. The Boys decoded it, and Adam read, "I have to go now, but remember that nothing is impossible."

"You're not leaving, are you, Violet?" asked Ray. "You can't leave. We need you."

Violet flashed and chimed lovingly, hovering in front of each boy for a few seconds. Then she flew into the hall and toward the front door. Ray opened the door and followed her into the yard. Violet rested a moment on Ray's shoulder, buzzed another short message, and rose into the air. She was still laughing in her merry way as she disappeared into the darkness above the trees.

"Why did you open the door for her? Why did you let her go?" asked Adam.

"Don't you see?" said Ray softly, still gazing into the darkness where Violet had disappeared. "She came to us by herself. I didn't find her—she came to me. And now she left by herself. It wouldn't be right to try to make her stay."

"She was just visiting, wasn't she?" said Adam.

"Yeah, just visiting," whispered Ray.

"What was her last message?"

"It was the same thing she said in my room," answered Ray. "I don't have to look it up. She said, 'Nothing is impossible.' "

On Monday, when Ray's parents signed the contract for the house, Ray was not even surprised when Mr. Miller presented them with a housewarming gift—a set of wind chimes for the front porch. Ray smiled to himself and thought, "Stranger things have happened."

All the rest of the summer and for many summers after that, when the evening breezes gently swayed the wind chimes on the porch, Ray heard again the merry sound of Violet's laughter.

Windchimes on the Porch

About the Author

Sharon Walrond Harris is a retired special education teacher and behavioral consultant. She has worked with students of all ages, from kindergarten through college level. She lives with her husband, Robert, in Noblesville, Indiana, and has two grown children and one grandchild.

Made in the USA
Charleston, SC
14 July 2016